MY TRIP TO THE
STONE AGE

by Vickie Saxon • illustrated by Kris Wiltse

Harcourt

Orlando   Boston   Dallas   Chicago   San Diego

Visit *The Learning Site!*

www.harcourtschool.com

October 3, 2323

Dear Diary:

Hello, my name is Louise. Today has been the most wonderful, spectacular, fabulous thirteenth birthday a *teenager* (yes, that's me!) could ever wish for! I got two really great presents. The first gift was you, a spacious new diary with exactly 124 empty pages to fill—that is, if I write on both sides of the paper, which I intend to do. The second gift was Nina Nanosecond, a highly advanced computer that will take me anywhere in time!

Nina resembles an enormous (well, five feet tall and four feet wide) black box on the outside, with a little door so that I can go inside whenever I feel like traveling through time. Nina also provides information about each time period—the people, the climate, the animals…I'm so excited to try her!

Oh, by the way, in case you're wondering about me, I am in sixth grade, exactly five feet tall, with curly black hair. My main interest is in history, especially *pre*-history (which, in case you didn't know, was the time before people were able to record the events of the time periods in which they lived). In fact, the first thing I plan on asking Nina is to show me all about the Stone Age, especially about its environment and how the geological shaping and changing of the Earth affected the way people lived.

Well, it's time for me to go now, but I will be sure to tell you everything that happens in my life, especially my exciting new adventures with Nina, the Stone Age, and more!

October 4, 2323

Dear Diary:

Today was an excellent day. Nina took me to the earliest part of the Stone Age, which is called the Old Stone Age. Even though the Old Stone Age lasted for an incredibly long period of time (about 3 million years!), Nina took me to a period that was close to the end of the Old Stone Age (about 35,000 B.C.). Nina told me (before we embarked on our trip, thank goodness!) that the Old Stone Age overlapped with the Ice Age—which meant that it was *extremely* cold!

The Old Stone Age
35,000 B.C.
Climate: Freezing

When Nina time-warped me back into the Old Stone Age, everything was covered in ice and snow. Since we were near the ocean, there was a wide beach. Nina explained that in northern parts of the world, the ocean water was covered with glaciers, gigantic pieces of ice that covered the land and sometimes, scouring the Earth's surface. She also told me that the seawater flowed from those areas down to the warmer areas farther south, bringing the cold water and glaciers with it.

Then Nina explained that the glaciers had been around from about 3 million years ago until about 10,000 B.C. Apparently people could walk between the continents without having to use a boat, because the sea level was lower, making more land and less water. The glaciers also provided icy routes for

people to travel between different lands. For example, our modern-day isle of Great Britain is separate from the rest of Europe, but in the Old Stone Age, it was connected by ice *and* by land because of a lower sea level!

The people I saw used small stone tools for domestic tasks, such as getting food and making clothes. They lived in caves, but they rarely stayed in one place, since they often had to travel in search of large animals for food. They did not grow plants, as we do now, because the climate was too cold and all the land was icy.

Europe as it looked during the Old Stone Age, when glaciers covered large areas of land and water

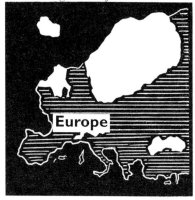

Europe

In the afternoon Nina took me to a later time in the Old Stone Age (about 10,000 B.C.). Even though it was a little bit warmer (a lot like what Alaska feels like these days), it provided an environment that required most people to continue being hunters and gatherers. This meant that the people hunted animals and gathered plants for food. Some areas of the world were warmer than others, because they were closer to the equator. The people there were able to survive better, because there were more available food resources and more accommodating weather.

I saw many large animals, such as reindeer, horses, bison, mammoths, and woolly rhinoceroses! These were the kinds of animals that flourished through the last part of the Ice Age due to their large size. Their bodies had a lot of fat to keep them warm and lots and lots of fur. These animals thrived on the grasses and mosses that grew on the wide, open plains during the late Stone Age, and they traveled in large herds. People hunted this source of food by living migratory lives following these animals.

Nina did make me feel a little better about the cold weather by explaining that there were greater temperature fluctuations between summer and winter during the Old Stone Age. It could be very cold in one area during the winter but almost comfortably warm during the summer months of the same year.

Well, I am very tired after my exciting day of traveling through time, but I do think I understand more about the Old Stone Age and how the environment affected the way people lived!

October 5, 2323

Dear Diary:

Today I visited the Middle Stone Age and acquired even more knowledge about the conditions of the times—the weather, the landscape, and the shape of the Earth's surface—and how they affected the way people lived. Nina showed me several times between the years 8000 B.C. and 7000 B.C., a much warmer era that came after the last of the Ice Ages, but before the time when agriculture became a regular part of how people subsisted.

I was able to witness the way people in the Middle Stone Age lived better lives than those in the Old Stone Age, because the climate had improved. I also saw how people living in the regions closer to the equator fared better than others, because they had more animals to hunt.

Nina explained that
the advent of the
Middle Stone Age
heralded warmer weather,
so the glaciers began to melt and
the seawater became warmer. This meant, of course, that sea
levels got higher, and the large beaches I saw in the Old
Stone Age began to disappear. Also, the land crunched up at
the same time, so the mountain peaks got higher. Overall,
the land became taller but smaller in area, and lakes and
ponds popped up where there once had been ice or flat,
grassy tundra.

I saw some dramatic floral changes, too, as trees became more abundant in the Middle Stone Age. There were mostly evergreen trees in the mountainous regions, but I also saw beech, oak, elm, and other types of trees in small patches around the lakes and smaller bodies of water that had appeared with the changes in the land. The growth of trees was the beginning of a dramatic change in the plant life of prehistoric ages. These trees preceded the growth of the forests and woodlands that would become significant during the environmental changes of the New Stone Age.

The changes in landscape, climate, and plant life also led to a change in the types of animals people hunted. Instead of giant fur-covered animals, I started to see slightly smaller animals that migrated less and traveled in smaller groups. These animals lived this way mainly due to the change in landscape, which now provided fewer open plains on which to graze. These newer animals included wild pigs, elks, and red deer, all of which seemed much smaller than the animals I had seen in the Old Stone Age. Nina also showed me that people began to train dogs, both as pets and as helpers in stalking and hunting animals. These same humans also developed traps to capture larger animals by digging out large pits.

Humans who lived near the oceans began to eat more fish as well as sea birds, and those who lived farther inland ate freshwater fish from the lakes and ponds. People also consumed many different types of food from plants, such as nuts, peas, lentils, and wheat.

Nina explained to me that people also began to change their tools, because of the changes in animals and the milder climate that produced more modern-looking landscapes. People created stone-tipped spears and used them to hunt and skewer the smaller animals that now populated the areas near their homes. Fishhooks were developed, as well as new-fangled contraptions, such as fish traps and nets.

Because of all of these changes, humans had more time for leisurely, sociable activities, such as creating art. I loved watching people decorate the walls of their caves, especially since their paintings looked a lot like the pictures of cave paintings we see in our modern museums.

October 6, 2323

Dear Diary:

Today Nina took me to the New Stone Age, which occurred between 7000 B.C. and 3000 B.C. She explained that this era marked the end of the Stone Age, because after this people began to make their tools out of metal.

In the New Stone Age, I learned that the climate warmed up so much that people began to live better, to undergo changes in their physical appearance (because they needed less hair on their bodies to keep them warm), and to change the ways in which they gathered their food staples. The biggest change in the New Stone Age was that humans finally became farmers. The result was more leisure time, a more reliable source of food, and better, longer lives.

During the New Stone Age, some people traveled north to familiar cold climates, while others remained farther south and enjoyed the new, warmer weather.

Great Britain

As the glaciers retreated, Europe began to appear as it does today.

The warmer weather created a huge change in the environment. As the forests spread, grassy plains were greatly reduced. Overall this change was bad for the large animals I had seen during the Old Stone Age, since they found it more difficult to survive in forests. On the open plains they had plenty of easily accessible grain to eat, and they could migrate much faster there as well. Groups of spear-bearing hunters had to track smaller animals through the forest areas, instead of finding a much easier target—large herds of animals grazing in the open grasslands.

On the other hand, I also noticed that some groups of people were able to move farther north during the New Stone Age, because it was warmer than it had been in the past. I guess you could say that some people wanted things to stay the same, so they moved north to climates with which they were familiar where they could continue hunting and gathering. Others enjoyed the warmer weather and adapted to the changes that came about with the growth of forests and other vegetation.

As I mentioned before, the warmer climate also allowed people to start farming—which meant they could stay in one place more easily by growing their food. They used more advanced stone tools, such as the sharpened pieces of rock they attached to long poles to make spears for hunting. They also attached heavy, sharply carved stones to shorter sticks to make axes and digging tools. However, I must say that if I had lived during this time, I would have developed a specialty in making decorative clay pots, since they were not only pretty but also useful for cooking and storing food.

Domesticated animals became a significant part of the lives and diet of people living in the New Stone Age; farmers of that time raised sheep, goats, cattle, and even pigs, just as our modern farmers do. They also grew delicious fruits, such as cherries and plums, in addition to staples such as wheat and other grains.

I must admit that the New Stone Age has been my favorite part of the Stone Age, simply because the lifestyle seems to have been luxurious compared to the frugal (and freezing cold) existence of humans in earlier times. Because people had learned to grow plants and raise animals to eat, and because they found ways of storing their food, they had more free time. They created more art and better homes, because they could live in one place instead of migrating in search of roaming beasts for food. They even created a new art by decorating their pottery, producing bowls and cups with both a functional and an ornamental use.

However, I must also add that I am astounded by (and have developed a tremendous respect for) all of our ancestors who lived in the different eras of the Stone Age. They had courage and intelligence, and they learned to adapt quickly and deftly to changes in their environment.